Fish & Soup

A Fish Tale

Story by Susan Sully

Illustrations by Tom Sully

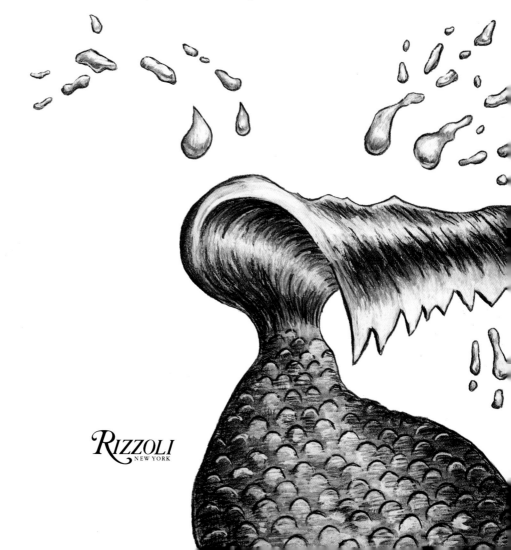

RIZZOLI
NEW YORK

First published in the United States of America in 1995 by
Rizzoli International Publications, Inc.
300 Park Avenue South
New York, New York 10010

Cataloging-in-Publication Data

Sully, Susan
Fish and Soup / story by Susan Sully; illustration by Tom Sully.
p. cm.
Summary: Henry Higginbotham feeds magic grow food to his fish,
and they attend a costume party as the Prince and Princess of Pescadoro.
ISBN 0-8478-1852-7
[1. Fish—Fiction. 2. Costume—Fiction.] I. Sully, Tom, ill. II. Title.
PZ7. S9538Fi 1995
[E]—dc20   94-32419
CIP
AC

Design by Douglas & Voss Group
Printed in Singapore

With love to Mom, Dad, Nancy, and Tom,
& special thanks to Lorraine, Pamela, Mary, Manuela,
Arthur, Eric, Sandy, Sarah, & Andrea (SS)

For fish out of water everywhere (TS)

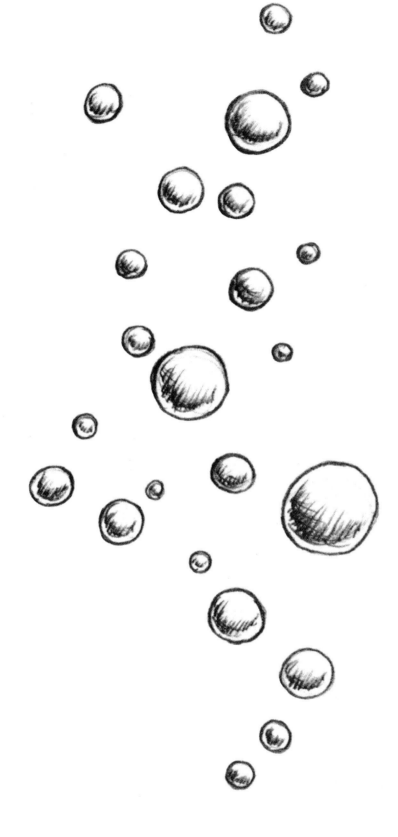

Henry Higginbotham kept hoping that Mephisto's Magic Grow Food would come by Friday. Then he could bring his pet fish along to Lady Chalmers' boring costume party.

On the night of the party, Henry put on his pirate costume and checked the mailbox one last time. The Magic Grow Food had arrived! He rushed into the house and emptied the packet into Glenda and George's bowl. Then he sat down to wait. Half an hour later, the Magic Grow Food *still* hadn't worked.

"Come on, Henry," his mother called. "If we don't leave now, we'll be late for the party!"

"Yeah, and a whole lot of fun that will be," Henry grumbled, glaring at Glenda and George. "Now I'll have to go without you."

Bang! The front door slammed shut. Glenda and George were all alone.

Drip. Drip. The water overflowed as the fish began to grow. They grew so big they popped right out of the bowl and landed with a splash on Mr. Higginbotham's favorite rug.

"Come on, George!" cried Glenda. "Let's go to the costume party!"

Slip, slish. Slip, slish. The two fish squished up the stairs to Mr. and Mrs. Higginbotham's room.

Glenda studied the contents of Mrs.
Higginbotham's closet. At last she saw the
perfect dress! She wriggled into it and wrapped a
ruby necklace around her neck. A splash of delicious French
perfume completed her costume.

"Ta da!" sang George as he spun through the room in a tuxedo.

Glenda gasped. How beautifully the black and white suit set off his silver scales!

Together they slid down the bannister and out the front door where the street lights shined on their shimmery tails.

"Ah, here you are at last," cried Lady Chalmers. "You must be the Prince and Princess of Pescadoro! What wonderful fish costumes! Do come in. We're about to serve the soup."

As the guests of honor, Glenda and George sat at the center of the table. When the soup was served, they stuck their heads right in and slurped. Everybody gasped . . . they had never seen such a thing before! How rude!

Always the perfect hostess, Lady Chalmers calmly said, "The Prince and Princess have traveled many miles to visit us from Pescadoro. Let us do everything we can to make them feel at home." Then she dropped her face into her bowl and drank. All the other guests did the same and soon the room was filled with the sound of slurping.

Henry, who was sitting way down at the end of the table, trained his telescope on the foreign guests.

"There's something fishy about that Prince and Princess," he thought.

"Jeepers!" he whispered. "It's Glenda and George!"

When the band began to play, everyone got up to dance.

"Oops!" cried Glenda as she tripped on her tail.

"Ooh la la!" yodeled George as he fell down beside her.

Together they wriggled and rolled on the floor in time to the beautiful tune.

"Look, a new dance!" shouted one of the guests.

"It's the Pescadoro Crawl!" screamed another.

Soon everyone was doing it. . . .

*P*lish, *plash.* Glenda and George heard the sound of running water.

"It's a fountain!" cried George, who had worked up quite a thirst. "Come on Glenda, let's get wet!"

And in they dove, tuxedo, tails, and all. The water felt so nice, they didn't even notice that the Magic Grow Food was wearing off.

"Yippee!" yelled Henry as he dove in after them.

"What a refreshing idea!" declared Lady Chalmers, pirouetting into the pool.

Before you could say "Pescadoro" three times, everyone was splishing and splashing in the fountain. Everyone, that is, except the Higginbothams, who thought things were going just a bit too far. . . .

"Henry!" called Mrs. Higginbotham, as she mopped a drop off her dress. "It's time to go home."

"Come on," Henry yelled to Glenda and George. But he couldn't find them anywhere.

Before Henry could say another word, his father pulled him out of the fountain and through the front door.

Henry shivered in his wet costume and worried all the way home. "What ever happened to Glenda and George?" he wondered. "How will they get home?" Suddenly Henry stopped in his tracks. "What if they never come back at all?"

Henry gazed mournfully at the empty fishbowl while his mother took off his jacket and hung it on a chair to dry. With a sigh, he climbed up the stairs and went to bed.

"What was that?"

Henry awoke with a start. Then he heard it again . . . a kind
of splashing sound. He ran to the parlor as fast as he could.

omething was moving in the empty fishbowl! Henry grabbed his telescope for a closer look. "It's Glenda and George!" he yelped.

For a moment, Henry wondered if he had dreamed the whole thing up. Suddenly something shiny caught his eye. It was Glenda's necklace . . . dangling from the pink pagoda! Just then George swam lazily into view and Henry was almost sure he saw him wink.